CW01678433

All's Fair in Love's War

All's Fair in Love's War

An A–Z of Open Combat

Nancy Linn–Desmond

POCKET BOOKS

New York London Toronto Sydney Tokyo Singapore

First published in Great Britain by Pocket Books, 1993
An imprint of Simon & Schuster Ltd
A Paramount Communication Company

Simon & Schuster Ltd
West Garden Place
Kendal Street
London W2 2AQ

Simon & Schuster of Australia Pty Ltd
Sydney

A CIP catalogue record for this book is available from the British Library.

ISBN 0-671-85113-6

Published by arrangement with Carol Publishing Group Inc,
600 Madison Avenue, New York, NY, USA

Previously published under the title:
Men Who Hate Women and the Women Who Hate Them.

Printed and bound by
HarperCollins Manufacturing, Glasgow

To Dad and Mom, who taught me the
importance of love and laughter;
To Sue, Bob, and Laura, who are always there
when I need a friend;
And to Dennie, who was well worth the wait.

DATING (dā' ting͡), 1. n. the process of spending enormous amounts of money, time, and energy to get better acquainted with a person whom you don't especially like now, but will learn to like a lot less.

Introduction

Are you a woman who believes that when a man says 'I love you', he means 'I love you'? That when he says, 'I'll call you later', he plans to call later? Or that, when he asks you to go out, he actually means for the two of you to go out?

Or perhaps you are a man who believes that when a woman says nothing is wrong, she means that nothing is wrong. That when she says she likes sports, she is referring to something other than talking on the phone and painting her fingernails. Or that when she suggests that the two of you talk honestly, she actually wants you to say what you think.

If so, you, like many men and women today, are a victim of the communication breakdown between the sexes. This dictionary is designed to help you correct your faulty assumptions about the opposite sex, while also familiarizing you with the rules and principles that govern feminine and masculine behaviour.

Within this book, women will find important information regarding their role in today's world, including such valuable guidelines as:

– How to get even with a man, even though you're not sure what transgression, if any, he has actually committed.

– How to use self-help quizzes in women's magazines to motivate yourself to end a happy relationship, quit a well-paying job, and otherwise disrupt your tranquil existence.
– How to apologize to a man, in a way destined to escalate any argument.
– How to use personal ads and dating services to locate men whom you would never, under any other circumstances, agree to date.
– How to take any statement made by a man and use it to start an argument.
– How to determine when a man, whose words and actions are only making you more miserable, is actually trying to comfort you.
– How to recognize when a man is engaged in sexual foreplay.

Meanwhile, male readers will also find important guidelines regarding their role in today's liberated relationships, including:
– How to lead an active single life, even though you are married.
– How to start an argument with a woman, without saying a single word.
– How to excel at such competitive masculine sports as eating, driving and joke-telling.
– How to compliment a woman in a way guaranteed to arouse her anger and irritation.
– How to convert telephones, barbecue grills and VCRs into instruments of torture.
– How to select furniture and pets designed to make any

woman, no matter how desperate, lose interest in living with you.

– How to tell if a woman, who hasn't even looked in your direction, is coming on to you.

Finally, it is the author's hope that, if nothing else, this book will at least accomplish two major objectives. First, that it will dispel those prejudices which block communication between the sexes, including the paranoid belief held by many women that, when a man is deliberately not telling the truth, he is lying.

And secondly, that it will broaden the reader's understanding of such essential relationship concepts as self-torture, sadistic revenge and public humiliation, without which one can never truly appreciate the masochistic art of dating.

A

A	a word that in a man's vocabulary is synonymous with several or many, as in 'stopping for *a* drink', 'eating *a* sandwich', and 'having *a* girlfriend'.
Accomplice	a man's best friend or business partner.
Adolescence	the period between puberty and maturity, characterized by extreme sexual preoccupation, moodiness and excessive partying. This period generally lasts from ages 12–21 in females and from ages 13–85 in males.
Alone	an adjective men use to describe a woman who is not with a man. Hence, a woman who is surrounded by several female friends may be asked by a man (who is neither blind nor on drugs), 'Are you alone?'

Alzheimer's Disease a condition characterized by an inability to remember such things as names, dates, phone numbers, etc. Once thought to affect primarily older people, recent evidence indicates that it has its most insidious effect on men in bars, many of whom are stricken overnight, leaving them unable to recall scheduled dates or to even remember the name or phone number of the woman with whom they spent the night.

Ambiguity a statement that is unclear or the meaning of which is uncertain. Men often make such statements in their conversations with women, as in the following examples:

The Man Says:	*The Woman Hears:*	*The Man Means:*
1. What are you doing later?	I'd like to take you to dinner.	If I don't find anyone I like better before the bars close, I'll come by your place and spend the night.

2. Don't go away.	I'll be right back.	Don't follow me. I'm trying to escape.
3. I feel so comfortable with you.	I love you already.	I think I'm falling asleep.
4. I know this sounds like a cliché but . . .	I care too much about you to lie to you.	It sounds like a cliché because it is one.

American Football a sport in which men try to score against an unwilling opponent and, in the process, do as much damage as possible to that opponent. After scoring, the men huddle together to congratulate each other on how tough, aggressive and ruthless they all are. Many people think that the sport of dating evolved from football.

Anxiety a feeling of dread and apprehension regarding the future. It is very similar to the feeling of being in love, the only distinguishing factor being that victims of anxiety don't enjoy the discomfort and try to avoid it.

Aphrodisiac something that turns a man on; this varies from man to man, though, in general, anything works if the woman is someone he barely knows, shouldn't be with and will probably never see again.

Apologize to end (or, more commonly, escalate) an argument by ostensibly taking the blame. Experts in the area (i.e., people who have spent a lot of time in male-female interactions) are able to make an apology in such a way as to cause the recipient of the apology to look like the guilty party and/or feel angrier than he or she did prior to receiving the apology. It is important to remember that the purpose of any apology is not to accept blame, but rather to make a sarcastic or disparaging comment and yet later be able to say, 'I apologized – what more do you want?' The following are examples of right ways and wrong ways to apologize to your mate:

Bad Apology:	*Good Apology:*
1. It was my fault	I'm sure it must be my

	fault – it usually is, isn't it? You never do *anything* wrong!
2. Please forgive me.	Well excu-u-u-u-se me!
3. I'm sorry.	I'm sorry if I didn't follow your orders to the letter, general!
4. I apologize.	I'm just sorry that you are so paranoid and so insecure that you can't look at this realistically.

Appetizer — the food that a man eats from his own plate, prior to eating the food from the plate of the woman with whom he is dining.

Argumentative — a word used to describe a woman who disagrees with a man.

Assertiveness a trait implying the tendency to speak up and take care of oneself. It is an important component of the new woman. Men state that they prefer assertive women 'up to a point'; this means that they like women to pay their own way but not to say what they really think.

Attraction the act of associating horniness with a particular person.

Attractive a term used to describe someone who is so unappealing that even in the throes of passion (or when desperately trying to get that person into bed), one cannot choke out the words 'gorgeous', 'beautiful', or even 'cute'. While not a favourite, women prefer the word 'attractive' to being called 'handsome', while men prefer it to being called 'interesting-looking'.

Available 1. a woman who is not married, engaged, or seriously involved with a man.
2. a man who is not dead.

B

Basketball	a sport in which a bunch of giants try to put a ball through a hoop; considering the height of each, the challenge is similar to an average-size person dropping a can into a waste basket. Men who like to watch this sport tend to like looking at hairy armpits.
Bed and Board	a man and woman living together; if married, known as 'bed and bored'.
Belch	a loud sound which a man rarely emits in the presence of a woman until after he is through trying to impress her. He then explains that such sounds are impossible for a man to control.
Binge	the eating behaviour of an over-weight man whenever his under-weight wife, who has been trying to help him diet by preparing nothing

Binge (cont'd.)	but low-calorie meals for the past six months, is out of the room.
Birth Control	avoiding pregnancy through such tactics as taking a pill, inserting a diaphragm and dating repulsive men.
Body Language	the belief that body movements and posture reveal feelings that are more honest than a person's verbalizations. Men are especially fond of interpreting body language, using the following guidelines to interpret a woman's movements:

Woman's Movement:	*Man's Interpretation:*
1. Crosses legs	'She wants me'
2. Scratches nose	'She wants me'
3. Crosses arms	'She wants me'
4. Walks across the room	'She wants me'
5. Sits down	'She wants me'

Boob Job	an expensive operation, which a woman undergoes in order to have larger breasts, so that she can later complain that men are only after her body.

Boobs	that part of a woman's anatomy which a man stares at while telling her how much he loves her eyes or her smile.
Braille	the type of reading referred to when a man is said to 'read a woman like a book'.
Breaking Up	1. the process of ending a relationship. 2. also, a woman's inability to contain her uncontrollable laughter when a man tells her, with tears in his eyes, that (a) the reason for 1. is because she's too good for him and (b) there is no other woman.
Briefcase	a case in which a man keeps all the important papers that he needs for work, including the funnies from the morning paper, information about ordering football match tickets, half-price lunch coupons, and business cards to pass out to any attractive women he meets on the way to or from work.
Broadminded	a term a man uses to describe himself. Women interpret it to mean

Broadminded (cont'd.)	that he is liberal or open-minded, while the man using the word simply means that he thinks about women a lot of the time.
Broker	1. a popular occupation, particularly among men; brokers are easy to recognize because they see everyone as a potential buyer or seller, judge the value of everyone and everything by how much someone else will pay for it, and refuse to take no for an answer. Their occupational title is indicative of their occupational goal: to make the rich broker and the broker rich. 2. also the financial condition of a man following a divorce.
Bypass	an alternate route to the toilet which may take a woman as much as twenty feet out of her way, while allowing her to walk past every attractive man in the room.

C

Call Waiting	a telephone feature that allows a single woman to put her friends, family and business associates on hold, while she responds to more vital or urgent calls, i.e., any call from a man.
Can Opener	1. the primary cooking utensil used by a man living alone. 2. a woman's role when watching *Match of the Day* with one or more men.
Car Phone	an expensive apparatus for transmitting static and portions of messages to a person a few miles away who thinks that he is receiving a transatlantic phone call from someone with a speech impediment.
Car Phony	a person who owns a car phone.
Castrating Bitch	a term used by men when referring to a woman who (a) refuses to go to

Castrating Bitch (cont'd.)	bed with a man or (b) goes to bed with a man who can't get it up.
Catty	a term used to describe a woman who makes derogatory statements about another person; a man who makes the same type of statement is called observant, witty or discriminating.
Celibacy	a word used to describe the sexual activity of single women who practise the 'safe sex' policy of limiting their sexual partners to men who are monogamous, honest and sexually responsible.
Comfort	to soothe or cheer a person who is feeling depressed. Men complain that most women are impossible to cheer up and, moreover, seldom appreciate a man's attempts to do so. For these women, who often even have difficulty telling when they are being comforted by a man, the following examples may be helpful:

Woman's Depressed Statement:	*Man's Statement of Comfort:*
1. I look so old. I'm only 35 but look	*Maybe we can get you an OAP discount at the cinema.*

at all the grey hair I'm getting.	
2. I don't have any friends. Nobody really cares about me.	*Think of all the money you'll save on Christmas presents.*
3. I hate that hairdresser! Be honest, doesn't my hair look hideously short?	*What hair?*
4. I think I may have AIDS.	*Well, you've been wanting to lose weight.*

Comfortable the primary requirement of a male shopper when buying either furniture or casual, at-home clothing. Generally, a man can quickly recognize a truly comfortable piece of furniture or clothing by the presence of the following features: (1) it is ugly; (2) it is too big for where he plans to put it; (3) it doesn't go with anything he already owns; and (4) his female companion, upon seeing it, immediately says, 'That is definitely the most hideous thing I've ever seen.'

Communication	a type of conversation that involves honest, open sharing of feelings and which ultimately leads to an argument.
Compatibility	the term used to describe two people who are tired of dating and, in an effort to avoid any more first dates, pretend for a while to like the same people, the same activities and each other.
Compliment	a statement of praise made by a man to a woman, which often goes unappreciated, thereby giving further support to men's contentions that 'women don't like to be treated nice'. Examples of unappreciated compliments include: 1. That dress does a great job of hiding fat thighs. 2. In that sweater, you almost look like you have boobs. 3. Compared to my ex-wife, even you are easy to get along with. 4. You're living proof that girls that aren't pretty try harder. 5. You're really not too stupid, for a woman.

Compromise	the method of conflict resolution in a relationship, whereby neither party gets what he or she wants, but each has the consolation of knowing the other one didn't either.

Contagious Enthusiasm	the tendency to get caught up in the excitement of another, thereby sharing with that person the emotion of the moment. One can generally determine how long a man and a woman have been dating by the level of contagious enthusiasm which they display, as in the following examples:

Statement:	*Response (if dating less than six months):*	*Response (if dating more than six months):*
1. 'My boss said that I'm getting a raise!'	'That's fantastic!'	'I hope you got it in writing.'
2. 'Did you see that goal?!'	'Yeah, wasn't that incredible?'	'I really don't care for football.'
3. 'Come here quick! I want you to see this!'	(Running into the room): 'Wow! That's really something!'	(Strolling into room five minutes later) 'You rang?'

Contagious Enthusiasm (cont'd.)

4. 'Don't you love this place? It's so romantic!'	'It's great and you look gorgeous by candlelight.'	'I hope you brought a flash light.'
5. 'Look at Fido! Isn't he some-thing?'	'He's adorable!'	'Does he *have* to lick himself like that.'

Contradict to assist one's date or spouse in relating a story or telling a joke.

Cover-Up 1. a conversation in which a group of men discuss, in the presence of their girlfriends or spouses, the important business deal which they were all working on until two a.m. the night before. 2. the attempt of a single woman to conceal from a new date, for as long as possible, such unattractive features about herself as her facial wrinkles, her flabby thighs, and her kids from a previous marriage.

Credit Cards a substitute for money, especially with single women, who determine their net worth by adding together the credit limits of all their credit cards.

D

Dating	the process of spending enormous amounts of money, time and energy to get better acquainted with a person whom you don't especially like now but will learn to like a lot less.
Dating Etiquette	widely accepted rules concerning various aspects of dating, generally involving one set of rules for men and another for women:

Category:	*Female:*	*Male:*
1. time of date	be ready one hour prior to the time set, but act like you're not ready when date arrives no matter how late he is.	on the first date, arrive within one hour of the time agreed upon; on subsequent dates, it's okay to be late.
2. dress	wear best dress, so that he will feel obligated to take you to a fancy, expensive place.	wear casual clothes so that no matter what she wears, you have an excuse

Dating Etiquette (cont'd.)		not to go to a fancy expensive place.
3. conversation	make sure he knows every intimate thing about you by the end of the evening, since the more he knows you, the more he loves you.	talk about sports and weather; don't give away any meaningful information about yourself, which could be used against you later (unless you are recently divorced, in which case spend the entire evening talking about your ex-wife and the divorce).
4. manners	it is okay to order a huge, expensive meal, as long as you don't eat it.	don't belch while kissing; don't drive off until she is all the way in the car; don't comment on her weight problem except in a nice

		way (e.g. you have skinny hair for a fat girl).
5. saying goodnight	throughout the evening, do everything you can to convince him that the two of you will have sex that night; then, at the end of the evening, slap his face when he attempts to kiss you, and slam the door in his face; men like women who are hard-to-get.	say it in bed, after sex.
6. if sex occurs	don't laugh when you see him naked; don't sing, 'Is that all there is?' or accuse him of never having done this before.	don't say, 'Boy how many times have you done this?' or, conversely, ask, 'Are you alive?'; don't introduce whips, chains and animals until the second encounter.

Dating Etiquette (cont'd.)

7. after sex	explain that you don't usually do this on the first date but he's special; try to make him feel responsible for you and guilty in advance if he's planning on not calling again.	say 'I'll call you'; try to get out of the door without kissing or touching her again.

Dating Quotient a quotient indicating a woman's potential for getting dates. The following equation is used to compute the dating quotient, with a quotient of 100 considered average:

$$DQ = \frac{(\text{chest size}) + (\text{no. of years under 30}) + (\text{no. of low-cut sweaters}) + (\text{no. of dates in past week})}{(\text{IQ score}) + (\text{no. children} \times 10)} \times 100$$

Dating Service an agency that for an exorbitant fee attempts to find the perfect mate for a female applicant, through the following sequential steps:
(a) having her fill out a detailed, extremely personal questionnaire;
(b) conducting a candid, often

embarrassing interview with her; (c) administering numerous tests to assess her personality and compatibility needs; (d) working with her to compile a profile of her ideal mate; and (e) fixing her up with either her ideal mate or the next male applicant to walk through the door, whichever of the two shows up first.

Dating Yourself 1. the act of giving away your age by admitting to remembering such things as hula-hoops, can-can slips and the band that Paul McCartney was with prior to Wings. 2. the act of going out with yourself, thereby only having to worry about your own desires, wishes and wants; many men make a habit of doing this while pretending to date a woman at the same time, in which case it is permissible for the woman to ask the man, the next time he invites her out, if it is okay if she brings a date.

Daydreaming a man's method of listening to that part of a conversation in which he is not doing the talking.

Defensive a descriptive term for a woman who

Defensive (cont'd.)	becomes annoyed when a man calls her fat or when a man she barely knows pats her on the bottom.
Delayed Reaction	the tendency of a man to put off laughing at a humorous comment or joke told by a woman, until that time in the future when he repeats it to her or somebody else.
Demanding	an adjective used by men to describe a woman who becomes angry when a man does not show up for their scheduled date.
Diaphragm	a device that a woman inserts shortly before sex to prevent pregnancy. While many women insert it improperly, it is nonetheless an effective method of birth control, since, by the time the woman finds it, prepares it, and inserts it, the man is sound asleep.
Dip	1. a movement in a dance, whereby a male unexpectedly lowers his partner toward the floor, causing her to lose her balance, bump into other dancers, and dislocate her back. 2. a man who does 1.

Directions something that a man who is driving will not stop to ask for until he has been lost at least two hours, has travelled more than 100 miles in the wrong direction, and has assured his female passenger at least thirty times that he knows exactly where he is.

Disregard the type of attention and consideration given by a man to a woman's opposing point of view.

Divorce and event that occurs when a man and woman have been married long enough to forget what dating was like.

Divorced previously married. Despite their bad press, people who have recently escaped from the institution of marriage are really no more disturbed or dangerous than anyone else who has recently escaped from an institution.

Doctor 1. a popular occupation often claimed by men trying to impress women in a bar; real doctors can be easily recognized by their lack of social skills and their tendency to ask

Doctor (cont'd.)	the waitress how much a drink costs prior to ordering one. 2. also, a verb describing what a doctor does, meaning to fix or alter, as in doctoring a tax return or a patient's bill.
Dog	man's best friend. For some unknown reason, most men seem to prefer dogs that are big, loud and immediately attempt to hump any woman who walks in the room; this preference is thought to have done much to advance the belief that dogs and their owners resemble each other.
Door	a large wooden board containing a knob on which a man hangs those clothes which are too expensive to be thrown on the floor.
Dragging Out	1. the act of forcing one's friends to go along on foraging expeditions to singles bars. 2. also, a man's method of telling a joke or relating a story.
Drunk	1. a man who is the life of the party. 2. a woman who is embarrassing her date.

E

Early	a man who arrives before 9:00 for an 8:00 date.
Easy	an adjective used to describe a woman who has the sexual morals of a man.
Embarrassment	a condition that exists when a woman does something which humiliates her date or spouse. The following is a list of common situations, along with a rating of each as a possible source of embarrassment for a man:

Situation:	*Embarrassing to Man?* Yes	No
1. Man looks down and sees that his fly is open		×
in the midst of making a speech to 1000 people.		×
2. Man's date states her opinion in front of man's family or friends.	×	

Embarrassment (cont'd.)	Yes	No
3. Man belches very loudly during quiet, solemn moment in movie or stage play.		×
4. Man's date complains of feeling ill and asks to leave party early.	×	
5. Nobody laughs when man tells long, drawn-out joke about an ethnic group, a member of which is seated at the table.		×
6. Man's wife or steady date wears skirt which reveals her knees in public.	×	

Emotion a feeling that a person experiences. For women, who have some difficulty interpreting the feeling behind a man's behaviour, the following table may be helpful:

Emotion:	*Man's Behaviour:*
1. sadness	cusses loudly; gets drunk
2. happiness	cusses loudly; gets drunk

3. anger	cusses loudly; gets drunk
4. frustration	cusses loudly; gets drunk
5. excitement	cusses loudly; gets drunk
6. love	cusses loudly; gets drunk

Emotional — a word used to describe a woman's tendency to be highly irrational and emotionally uncontrolled, as opposed to a man's tendency to exhibit rational, well-controlled behaviour. An example of a woman's emotional nature is a woman who is unable to refrain from crying after a man who just saw his team lose on *Match of the Day* throws a chair through her TV set.

Engagement — a period of time prior to marriage, during which the woman looks for the perfect dress and the man looks for a way out.

Entrepreneur — a popular occupation of men in bars, usually synonymous with the terms 'unemployed', 'bankrupt' and 'bullshit artist'.

Eulogize — to discuss a former girlfriend or ex-wife with one's new girlfriend. It is

Eulogize (cont'd.)	customary for the man delivering the eulogy to don a faraway look, emit a nostalgic sigh, and make a statement such as 'Susan was a beautiful girl', leading the female listener to wonder if Susan is dead or if she just suddenly got ugly.

Excerpt	a portion of a statement that is taken out of context so that the listener hears only what he wants to hear or later quotes only the portion of the statement that supports his position, as in the following examples:

Statement:	*Excerpt as Used later:*
1. 'Go ahead and do it if you don't mind ruining our whole relationship.'	'You said go ahead and do it.'
2. 'You may be sexy, but you're also self-centred, spoiled, and insensitive.'	'You think I'm sexy?'
3. 'Just don't bother coming over; it's obvious that you don't care about me	'*You*' told me not to come over – how was I supposed to know that you really wanted me to?'

and that the fact that I love you and miss you means nothing to you.'	
4. 'I expect, if you didn't love me anymore and told me that you never wanted to see me again, then I expect I'd go out with somebody else, but my heart wouldn't be in it.'	'What did you expect me to do? *You* started it! *You* were the one that said you were going out with somebody else.'

Example an illustration used by a man to explain some generalization which he has just made; while, to a woman, the connection may at first seem far-fetched, with further explanation from the man, she comes to realize that it makes no sense at all.

Exclamation Point the punctuation used at the end of a statement denoting strong emotion. It indicates that the speaker is either gasping, shouting, groaning or crying, and is the punctuation most commonly used by a woman communicating with a man.

Excuse (cont'd.)	a woman's role when a man is trying to avoid a commitment which he previously made; for some reason, in such instances, men feel more comfortable lying about their date's physical health than about their own.
Expert	a man's status on any subject being discussed.
Ex-wife	a woman whom a man divorced, after deciding that getting rid of the arguments about money, kids and each other's bad habits was worth the considerable financial cost, and with whom he now spends a great deal of time arguing about money, kids and each other's bad habits.
Exwifephobia	1. a condition in which a man experiences intense feelings of panic and anxiety, along with extreme avoidance tendencies, whenever forced to deal with his ex-wife. In severe cases, the anxiety reaction may also occur when he hears the words alimony, child support or lawyer, and when he sees a car, house or dog similar to the one he

owned prior to the divorce; in such cases, he may also show a pathological avoidance of any person whom he judges to be as greedy, vicious and potentially dangerous as his ex-wife (i.e., any woman). 2. a similar reaction in a woman dating a divorced man. It is manifested by the woman avoiding any situations or activities where the ex-wife or something that belongs to her (e.g., wedding pictures, alimony cheques, old letters, hostile kids, etc.) may be encountered. In severe cases, the woman may even begin to avoid such previously enjoyable activities as snooping in the man's desk drawer, listening in on his phone calls, reading his mail, and going through his wallet and chequebook. 3. also, a condition in which a married woman becomes extremely fearful that her husband may leave her, thereby forcing her to get a job, lose weight and go to singles bars.

Eye Contact a method utilized by a single woman to communicate to a man that she is interested in him. Despite being advised to do so, many women have

Eye Contact (cont'd.)	difficulty looking a man directly in the eyes, not necessarily due to shyness, but usually due to the fact that a woman's eyes are not located in her chest.

F

Fable a story with a moral. Women are fond of using them, either in fictional or historical form, to try to subtly teach a man a lesson. This is seldom successful, since most men have as much difficulty sorting out a woman's hidden message in a story as they do in real-life conversations with her, particularly if her message conflicts with their pre-existing beliefs:

Synopsis:	*Man's Interpretation of Moral:*
1. Popular Fable: three pigs build houses; the one that invests the most time and effort ends up with the house that is the most effective in protecting him from	It's a dangerous world, especially for pigs and homeowners.

Fable (cont'd.)	the wolf who destroys the other two houses and eats the other two pigs.	
	2. Popular Fable: a dog sees a magnified reflection in the water of the bone he holds in his mouth; thinking that the reflection is a real bone, he attempts to get it and in the process drops the real bone in the water, ending up with nothing.	Life isn't fair – somebody's always trying to trick you.
	3. Real Life Event: a man takes his girlfriend for granted; he neglects her and chases other women. Eventually, he loses her and finds out, too late, that she was exactly what he was looking for all the time.	Women can't be trusted.

Fashion Statement a message about a person, which is conveyed to others by the styles and fashions adopted by that person. Such statements are particularly prevalent in singles bars, including the following examples:

MEN

Style:	*Statement:*
1. wears sunglasses indoors or else places them on top of head or on chain or string around neck; wears gold chains.	'I'm a jerk.'
2. wears white patent leather shoes and belt; slicks hair down in wet look; wears leisure suit.	'I love watching wrestling, dancing the polka, and listening to Slim Whitman.'
3. wears Polo shirts and Rolex watch; carries key chain which identifies car as Porsche or Mercedes.	I'm either rich or, more likely, up to my ass in debt.'
4. wears beeper; carries briefcase;	'I wish I were important or,

Fashion Statement (cont'd.)	always appears to be in a hurry.	at least, had a job.'
	WOMEN	
	Style:	*Statement:*
	1. wears tight-fitting jumpsuit; has 4" high heels and 3" red acrylic fingernails.	'Whatever you want, the answer is yes.'
	2. wears tennis dress with matching head-band or tights and leotards with match-ing sweatband.	'I look so cute in this get-up that I'm cer-tainly not going to do anything to get it all sweaty.'
	3. wears short ruffled skirt and long, long, hair, regardless of age.	'It's more important to look young than to look good.'

Fast Forward a VCR control that allows the viewer to save time through bypass-ing the boring portions of a movie and going directly to its highlights. Through the use of this feature, the male viewer is able to quickly advance to those scenes in which violence, nudity or sex are featured, while avoiding scenes which are needlessly bogged down with any semblance of meaningful dialogue or plot development.

Fat unsightly excess weight on a woman; on a man, this is called brawn or the man is referred to as 'big' or 'a bull'. It is particularly important to note that the watermelon-size bulge in a man's stomach, often referred to as a beer belly or gut, has absolutely *nothing* to do with being fat and, in fact, is considered by most men to be the only infallible way to discriminate real men from fags.

Faults behaviours in a woman that are in conflict with the personality of the man she is dating, as in the following examples:

Woman Described As . . .	*Man Is Probably . . .*
compulsive spender	stingy
jealous	unfaithful
impatient	chronically late/slow moving
unsociable	excessive party-goer

Faults (cont'd.)

untrusting	untrustworthy
nymphomaniac	impotent
frigid	sexually unskilled
hyperactive	lazy
intellectual snob	stupid

Fickle a word used to describe a woman who gets tired of a man before he gets tired of her.

Fifth Wheel a woman who is out with a man and his best friend.

Fix to do irreparable damage to something which previously had a slight malfunction or unnoticeable flaw, as in a man making household repairs.

Flexibility the tendency of today's liberated male to be more accepting of a woman's individual differences and less rigid regarding her physical appearance. Hence, while males in the sixties and seventies may have sought physical perfection in their mates, today's male is willing to accept a number of imperfections in a female partner, including such deviations as legs that are too long, hair that is too shiny and breasts that are too large.

Fondaphobia a condition of intense anxiety and avoidance in women, created by over-exposure to Jane Fonda Workout tapes. In extreme cases, the anxiety reaction occurs not only when watching the tapes, but also whenever the Fondaphobic is exposed to skinny thighs, people made of rubber, reruns of *On Golden Pond* and any activity requiring pelvic thrusts. Since many experts believe that the best way to overcome a phobia is to pair the anxiety-provoking event with a pleasurable event, people treating Fondaphobics often advise a regimen in which the Workout tapes are watched while simultaneously eating ice cream, biscuits, sweets, etc. By applying the directions given on the tape to eating rather than exercising, these victims in time learn to feel happy and excited, rather that fearful and depressed, when they hear Jane tell them 'faster, faster', 'lift it up', 'in-out', and 'one more time'.

Football a sport that men appreciate because it involves two of their favourite pastimes – kicking and spitting.

Foreplay 1. activity that precedes sexual intercourse. While methods vary, most males prefer to limit themselves to the basic three-step approach to foreplay, consisting of (1) taking off their pants, (2) crawling into bed, and (3) turning out the light. 2. a man's interpretation of any touch from a woman.

Friend 1. a person of the same sex, with whom an individual spends a great deal of time until one of them gets married and disappears. 2. also, a member of the opposite sex who is unattractive or has some other flaw which makes sleeping with him totally unappealing.

Friendly the term a man uses to describe his attention to an attractive woman; the same level of friendliness toward a member of the opposite sex, when exhibited by a woman, is referred to as flirting or coming-on.

Frigidity a term used by men to describe a female sexual dysfunction, in which a woman fails to become excited and/or to have an orgasm at the time and place which is most convenient for her male partner.

G

Gay those men in a singles bar who are the best-looking, best-dressed and best-groomed.

Geographically Undesirable a term used by a man to describe a woman who is not a good dating prospect because she is either more than a 15-minute drive away or else lives near enough to see what time he comes home and with whom.

Getting Even an important element in all successful relationships; it involves paying back one's partner for any real or imagined slight and is based upon the rule, 'Do unto others as they have done unto you, are planning to do unto you, or may have possibly done unto you without your knowing it.' The following are examples of ways to successfully interpret a man's actions and decide upon an appropriate way of getting even, thereby gaining his respect and

Getting Even (cont'd.) ultimately strengthening the relationship:

Man's Action:	*Interpretation:*	*Get-Even Tactic:*
1. doesn't call one evening.	he's out with another woman.	go to bed with his best friend.
2. yawns.	he's getting bored.	tell him you never want to see him again.
3. brings flowers.	he's feeling guilty.	throw the flowers at him and slam the door in his face.
4. says, 'I love you.'	he's trying to trick you.	laugh at him – if possible, in front of friends.
5. plans an expensive vacation for the two of you.	he wants you out of town until his latest indiscretion blows over.	wait until the last minute, when it's too late for a refund, and then refuse to go.

Glare the affectionate way a woman watches her date when he is either

	telling a group of people about her most embarrassing moment, instructing her in front of friends on how to improve herself, or spending the entire evening making sure that the most attractive woman at his party doesn't 'feel left out'.
Gossip	what women do when they talk with each other. When men do the same thing it is called 'conferring', 'discussing' or 'consulting'.
Gourmet	a man who uses Dijon mustard on his hot dog.
Grovelling	the behaviour referred to when a woman tells a man that all she wants is a 'simple apology'.
Guessing Game	an activity wherein a woman acts angry and her partner attempts to discover the source of her anger. This is an especially useful game for a woman who is in the mood to argue but can't think of a good topic, as it places the responsibility on the man, who must then run through a list of his wrong-doings, from which the woman selects one

Guessing Game (cont'd.)	or more which she considers suitable for an argument.
Gullible	a word used to describe a woman who believes something that a man tells her. The following examples illustrate the way to replace gullible responses with more correct responses and thereby avoid (a) being labelled gullible and (b) wasting time on insincere men who, when repeatedly confronted with non-gullible responses to their tactics, will immediately move on to less perceptive women:

Man's Statement:	*Gullible Response:*	*Correct Response:*
'I'll see you at 8:00.'	'Okay.'	'And who are you seeing at 7:00.'
'I have to work late tonight.'	'Okay.'	'Sure you do – if you call getting in to your secretary's knickers work.'
'It was a wrong number.'	'Oh.'	'Don't give me that. I'm

		not stupid. I know what's going on.'
'I would just like to spend a quiet night at home alone with you.'	'Okay.'	'Are you afraid we'll run into one of your other girl-friends if we go out, or are you just too cheap to spend any money on me.'
'Good-night.'	'Good-night.'	'It probably will be for you – now that you're getting rid of me and can go to meet *her*.'

H

Half-Baked	1. a man's opinion of a woman's brilliant idea, prior to the time that he presents it to others as his own. 2. a style of cooking practised by men and many single women, in which food is cooked to a level of doneness described as rare, including steaks and beefburgers, but also eggs, coffee, biscuits, and cake.
Hangover	the price one pays for insisting on staying at a singles bar until he or she meets somebody who seems attractive and appealing – a task which generally is impossible without consumption of excessive amounts of alcohol. People who have experience with these type of endeavours contend that the best way to quickly determine how bad a hangover is going to be is, upon waking the next morning, to immediately roll over and see how unattractive the person sleeping beside you is.

Health	1. a reason for happiness used by a person grasping at straws while attempting to cheer up a friend who is going through a painful divorce or break-up, as in, 'You still have your health'. It is seldom effective since the only people who realize its importance are the ones who don't have it. 2. a class in school where it first becomes evident that the whole male-female thing is not going to be easy.
Heartbroken	a condition affecting the rejected party in a broken relationship; this condition in a woman usually lasts several months, while in a man it lasts up to the time that another woman smiles at him.
Hen-Pecked	a word men use to describe a man whose relationship with a woman is characterized by such grossly unacceptable behaviours as returning her phone calls, remembering her birthday and showing up for their scheduled dates.
Historical Fiction	a story based loosely on reality, wherein the places and people are

real but the events are altered in order to make the story more interesting, more emotional, and more in keeping with the author's viewpoint – as in a person discussing a past relationship or failed marriage.

Hobby a conversational category in interviews by potential employers and dates, designed to weed out those candidates who are not appropriately interesting, active, and talented. When a man asks a woman what her hobby is, it must be remembered that there are certain right and wrong answers and that the answer given should be based on what sounds good rather than what she actually enjoys doing. Wrong answers include watching TV, eating, knitting, sleeping, talking on the phone and spending a man's money. Right answers include tennis, skiing, sky-diving and running. It is often helpful for the woman, when making up an answer which sounds good, to also make up a reason why she can regrettably no longer engage in this hobby (which she has never really engaged in

Hobby (cont'd.)	anyway); this prevents embarrassment later when the man suggests that the two of them share the hobby. An example is a woman saying that she loves sky-diving but no longer engages in it because her fiancé was killed when the two of them were sky-diving together last year. (This is an especially good response, as it also fulfils another date-screening requirement – that the woman explain why she is not now and/or has never been married.)
Holiday	the act of spending a lot of money and travelling a long distance in order to have new surroundings in which to fight.
Honesty	a trait associated with people who have few friends and fewer dates.
Hunk	a man who looks like Tom Selleck or Robert Redford; also, a man who looks like Rupert Murdoch but owns a multi-million pound corporation.
Hypothetical Question	a question based on a hypothetical event, wherein the person who

answers is usually expected to tell what he would do were a certain situation to exist. This type of questioning is generally a foolproof way to start an argument, particularly if the person posing the question is careful to select one to which any answer could conceivably be wrong, as in the following example:

QUESTION: If you had an affair, would you tell me?

Male's Response:	*Appropriate Rebuttal:*
1. No.	That's just great. Not only would you cheat, you'd also lie! What kind of a jerk are you?
2. Yes.	You'd tell me something like that, knowing that it would destroy me and our whole relationship? I can certainly see how much I mean to you!
3. I'd never have an affair with anyone else.	The question is: *if* you did. Why can't you just answer the question? Obviously, you're afraid that something might slip out that you're trying to hide from me! What is it? And don't say 'nothing'!

I

I'll Call You a phrase frequently used by a man following an encounter with a woman, particularly if sex was involved in the encounter; it is often substituted for more accurate (but less acceptable) phrases, such as 'how did I get myself into this' and 'let me out of here'. The preceding phrase 'don't call me' is often implied though not stated (as in, 'Don't call me – I'll call you').

I Love You an overused phrase in relationships, generally having more to do with the needs of the speaker than with the feelings toward the recipient. The phrase is often substituted for 'I'm horny', 'I'm sorry' and 'I'm hungry'.

Imaginative a word used to describe a person, particularly in personal ads. Men who describe themselves as imaginative in such ads tend to expect their

Imaginative (cont'd.)	partners to incorporate costumes, acrobatics and animals into the sexual act.
Incompatibility	the condition that arises when two people who have totally different values and interests, i.e., a man and a woman, try to live together. While present from the outset, it does not usually become an important issue until the initial lust has worn off.
Indecisive	a person who is separated but not divorced . . . or divorced but not separated.
Indifference	a woman's feeling toward a man, which is referred to by the man as 'playing hard to get'.
Individuality	the quality that makes a person independent in his behaviour, unique in his thinking, strong in his personal beliefs and impossible to live with.
Inferiority Complex Complex	a complex based on principles found in such popular self-help books as *I'm OK . . . You're OK*; it is a condition in which a person who is

markedly inferior convinces himself that his inferiority is imaginary. This complex has wreaked much havoc on the singles scene, as it has resulted in an excess of unattractive, unappealing people who, rather than recognizing their limitations and potential, now force themselves, in an aggressively self-assured manner, on disinterested, disgusted members of the opposite sex.

Innocence the appealing trait of wide-eyed naïveté in an unknown woman, which in a man's date or spouse is referred to as stupidity.

Interesting a word a man uses to describe a woman who lets him do all the talking.

Interests hobbies or pastimes that two people in a relationship share in an enjoyable way for approximately one to three months; at that time one of the following things happens to dampen their enthusiasm: (a) one partner, having surpassed the other, tries to instruct the other, (b) one partner, having been surpassed by the other, tries to instruct the other, or (c) one partner refuses to participate any longer because the other displays annoying habits when engaged in the hobby, usually including being a poor winner, showing-off or appearing overly humble after a victory, or winning repeatedly due to luck rather than skill. Despite its short-lived success, many people continue to believe that it is important for a couple to initially share a number of interests; these same people wrongly contend that desperate people will settle for partners with whom they have nothing in common. This kind of thinking is typical of the widespread, unfair prejudice against desperate people; in reality, studies show that not only do desperate people require five mutual interests in potential partners (as do their non-desperate counterparts), but they often select interests that last longer, as in the following examples:

Non-Desperate:	*Desperate:*
1. we both play tennis.	1. we both breathe.

	2. we both dance.	2. we both are alive.
	3. we both ski.	3. we both used to be younger.
	4. we both like movies.	4. we both have pimples.
	5. we both like football.	5. we both like him.

Interrogator a woman's role when listening to a man discuss money, other women or what he does when she's not there.

Introductory Clause a phrase frequently used when conversing with members of the opposite sex, to introduce a sentence that will subsequently prove to be in direct opposition to the intent or sentiment expressed in the introductory clause. Such misleading clauses include, 'To tell you the truth . . . ', 'To make a long story short . . . ' and the ever-popular 'I don't mean to start an argument but . . .'.

Irreconcilable Differences legal grounds for ending a marriage, based on the determination that

Irreconcilable Differences (cont'd.)	certain important conflicts between a married couple cannot be resolved. Generally, the notion of irreconcilability varies from couple to couple and is largely a function of other, unstated factors – in particular, the physical attractiveness of one's partner. For example, a man married to a gorgeous, sexy woman may consider her paranoid schizophrenic tendencies and numerous episodes of chasing him with a butcher knife to be irreconcilable only if he is a high-strung haemophiliac with a heart condition. Meanwhile, a man married to an ugly woman may list such irreconcilable differences as (a) 'she wakes up five minutes before I do in the morning', (b) 'I weigh more than she does', (c) 'I don't like the way she breathes' and (d) 'I say potato – she says potäto'.
Irritating Habits	what the endearing little qualities that initially attract two people to each other turn into after a few months together.

J

Jack 1. a mechanical device that men use to raise a car when changing a flat tyre. In a woman's car, the jack is generally found in the trunk underneath the suitcases, books and shopping bags, near the area where the spare tyre was stored before being removed to make room for more essential items. 2. the 'hero' in the nursery rhyme 'Jack and Gill', who first introduces little girls to the hazards of asking an unwilling male to help out with household chores.

Jacuzzi a type of bathtub to provide a way for the owner to insist that his female guests disrobe, without seeming lecherous and also without even having to use romantic lines. Men who have Jacuzzis also tend to have (a) more than one girlfriend, (b) a Polaroid camera, (c) three or more gold chains and (d) an

Jacuzzi (cont'd.)	exaggerated idea of how good they look in the nude.

Jealousy irrational, unjustified suspiciousness regarding the relationships of one's partner with members of the opposite sex. The following questions are designed to allow any woman to determine whether, from the male perspective, she and/or her man are overly jealous. The sets of questions differ somewhat, as the same traits that in a woman reflect paranoid jealousy are often, in a man, signs of a perceptive, astute individual.

WOMAN'S TEST

0–1 Yes answers = moderately jealous
2 Yes answers = extremely jealous
3 Yes answers = pathologically jealous

1. Have you ever in your life been suspicious, for even a moment, of a man's motives? [This applies to *any* man, including business figures (like Robert Maxwell) and fictional characters (such as J. R. Ewing).]

2. Would you be annoyed (even slightly) if you were at a party with a date who spent the entire evening talking with another woman and eventually left the party with her, forcing you to find another ride home?

3. If a man broke a date with you, telling you that he was hospitalized with a serious illness, and you saw him out with another woman that same evening, would it cross your mind that he had possibly lied to you?

MAN'S TEST

0-1 Yes answers =	non-jealous
2 Yes answers =	overly protective
3 Yes answers =	mildly jealous

1. Have you, in the past month, attempted to kill a man you thought was looking at your date? (It doesn't count if she looked at him also, in which case you were provoked and not responsible for your behaviour).

2. Have you ever gone to a former girlfriend's wedding and attempted to shoot her and her new husband?

Jealousy (cont'd.) (It doesn't count if she invited you or told you that she was getting married, in which case you were provoked and not responsible for your behaviour.)

Joint Decision 1. the decision-making process in modern man-woman relationships, whereby decisions regarding the relationship, rather than being made by the man alone, are now discussed and mutually agreed upon by the man and his drinking buddies. 2. one of the many types of important decisions that men working together must discuss and agree upon each day, including where to go for lunch, what chocolate bars to have put in the snack machine, and what pub to go to after work.

Joke-Telling a competitive male sport in which various joke-telling skills are displayed and evaluated in areas including velocity, frequency and variability, as well as content, punch-line quality, and laughter response. The following rules and definitions apply to the various categories:

1. Velocity: speed of delivery; unlike most other sports, skill in joke-telling is measured by a *decrease* in velocity; most even moderately skilled joke-tellers are able to spend 5–10 minutes telling a 30-second joke.

2. Frequency: the number of times a joke-teller repeats the same joke; a high frequency is the goal, with extra points given for each time the joke is told in the presence of the same person (usually the joke-teller's steady girlfriend or spouse); it should also be remembered that one of the reasons for re-telling any joke is to find a way to each time make it a little longer.

3. Variability: the ability to vary a joke; the goal is to be able to take any joke just told by an opponent, claim to have heard it 'a little differently', and retell it in such a way that it is even longer than the joke initially presented by the opponent.

4. Content: to experienced joke-tellers, there are only two acceptable

Joke-Telling (cont'd.)

content categories: (a) sexually disgusting jokes and (b) jokes which make fun of specific groups of people, preferably in which the joke-teller can imitate dialects, accents and speech impediments; hence, a joke about an Italian harelip and Irish stutterer would be considered a good joke. It is perfectly acceptable – even desirable – for a joke-teller to find a way to incorporate dialects, accents and speech impediments into any joke, even when their presence has absolutely nothing to do with the point of the joke; in fact, by doing so, extra points are often earned in the categories of Variability and Velocity.

5. Punch Line: the quality of the punch line is not measured by how funny it is but by how long it occurs after the first line of the joke; by the time a really experienced joke-teller gets to the punch line, most listeners have forgotten (and/or don't care) how the joke began.

6. Laughter: the goal in this category is for the joke-teller to laugh

louder and longer than any of his listeners; this is particularly effective if he can manage to refrain from laughing at all, in response to jokes told by anyone but himself.

Jumping to Conclusions	an activity a woman engages in that totally disrupts her otherwise stable, happy relationship with a man. It involves blowing relatively minor events totally out of proportion. An example is a woman finding her boyfriend in bed with a naked lady and jumping to the conclusion that they were having sex.

K

Keepsake	a memento kept for sentimental reasons. Women tend to feel particularly sentimental during a break-up or divorce and often wish to keep items that remind them of happier times, including the house, the cars and the money.
Killjoy	a woman who refuses to go along with the harmless pranks her date and his friends are planning, including mooning motorists in passing cars, entering her in a wet T-shirt contest and setting her dog on fire.
Kleptomaniac	a person who has an irresistible urge to steal something that is of questionable value, is neither wanted nor needed, and for which, after the theft, the person has little use, as in a woman stealing another woman's husband.
Know-how	a man's knowledge of how to do

Know-how (cont'd.)	something, such as cooking, wall papering and working on cars; generally referred to as 'no-how' by his victims.
Know-it-all	a woman who claims to have some piece of knowledge that her date doesn't.

L

Lack of Communication	the typical conversation between a man and a woman.
Late	a man's estimated time of arrival for a date.
Laughter	a sound produced by one member of a heterosexual couple, while the other member looks on in a bored or irritated manner. The likelihood of a man and woman ever actually laughing at the same time is slim, but it can happen if events are carefully orchestrated and if simple modifications are made, as in the following examples:

Situation:	*Will Man Laugh?*	*Will Man's Girlfriend Laugh?*
1. man pulls chair out from under a person	Yes	No

Laughter (cont'd.)

. . . to whom he was once married or engaged.	Yes	Yes
2. man tells harelip joke	Yes	No
. . . to an attractive female who, prior to seeing this side of his personality, had been making a play for him.	Yes	Yes
3. man's girlfriend tells joke	No	Yes
. . . while trying to decide whether she's in a good enough mood to have sex.	Yes	Yes

---

Law of Relationships the less you care about a given man, the harder he is to get rid of.

Law of Relative Humidity the principle that allows one to predict the amount of moisture that will be in the air at any particular time. This law states that the relative humidity will rise proportionate to two factors:
(a) the frizzability of a woman's hair

	and (b) the importance of the outdoor event which she is attending.
Law of Relativity	how attractive a given man appears to be is directly proportionate to how unattractive your date is.
Lawyer	a popular occupation that a man often falsely attributes to himself in order to impress women in bars. It is difficult to discriminate real lawyers from impostors, since nobody knows what (if anything) lawyers really know. However, some women claim to be able to recognize true lawyers by their outstanding verbal faculties (meaning they sound very intelligent while saying nothing).
Leading a Man On	an act associated with a woman who uses such obvious come-ons as looking attractive, walking past a man, and looking at him when he yells out her name, but then refuses to go to bed with him.
Lecture	a man's response to a simple yes-no question posed by a woman seeking advice or information on a subject

Lecture (cont'd.)	which she finds boring, such as insurance, car repairs and electrical engineering.
Left Hand	the hand that every married man in a singles bar keeps in his pocket.
Leftovers	that which has not been eaten at the conclusion of a meal. If a man is present at the meal, leftovers usually consist of the plates, the napkins and the silverware.
Liberated Male	a man who no longer clings to the macho male image but instead is willing to offer assistance on tasks previously relegated solely to females. For example, while a macho male refuses to offer to help with the dishes, a liberated male is often heard to say to a woman, just as she finishes doing the dishes, 'Hon, can I help you with the dishes in there?'
Love	a feeling for another person, meaning that you would rather be treated badly by him than by anyone else.
Love at First Sight	what occurs when two extremely horny people meet.

Lunch Date a suspicious type of date, made by a man who obviously isn't free in the evenings. While most women consider it a tip-off that the man is either (a) married, (b) living with a woman or (c) involved in underworld crime, optimistic women often agree to the date and hope for (c).

M

Make-over 1. to make a big deal about somebody, such as a man and a woman, who have just met, making over each other. 2. the next step in a relationship, following (1) above, in which the partners try to change those traits in each other that they initially liked. 3. a popular service offered at beauty shops and department stores, wherein every woman, regardless of how she looks when she arrives, is made over into a style that looks like a cross between Bette Midler and Glenda the Good Witch from *The Wizard of* Oz.

Make-up 1. something that a man tells a woman she doesn't need, until he sees her without it. 2. the point in an argument at which horniness and desperation overcome pride and principles.

Manic-depressive	the mental condition of a person who has just fallen in love.
Masochist	a woman who dates often, goes to singles bars frequently, and lives in a singles apartment complex.
Masquerade	to get ready for a date or a trip to a singles bar.
Mature	a word used to describe a man who has reached the age at which a woman is called old.
Meeting the kids	an event occurring approximately six months after a woman's first date with a divorced man and often simultaneously with their last date. Highlights of the event include the kids reminiscing with Daddy about family vacations and reminding him of all Mummy's good points; when the kids interact at all with Daddy's girlfriend, it is usually to ask how much every piece of jewellery she's wearing costs and if Daddy bought it for her, to comment on something about her that looks funny, and to scream or cry whenever Daddy touches her.

Women who have survived such meetings state that the most important prerequisite to passing the meet-the-kids test is being able to smile through anything; appropriate practice exercises include forcing oneself to smile during gum surgery, blind dates and reruns of the Three Stooges.

Memory 1. a cognitive function that is inconsistent or absent in men, accounting for a man's inability to remember such things as a woman's birthday, the time that he's due for a date and the fact that he's married. 2. an overdeveloped cognitive function in women, allowing a woman to recall in detail every minor transgression ever committed by any man with whom she is now, or was at one time, romantically involved.

Midlife Crisis the condition of horniness, dissatisfaction and greed that exists throughout life, but which is assigned a name during one's thirties and forties.

Mislay 1. to misplace something, as in a woman hanging up a man's tie or putting his coat in the closet. Due to such infuriating behaviour on the part of women, the first thing a man does when he is looking for anything (from his football to his variable speed reversible drill) is to ask the woman where it is. A man can always tell that a woman is really itching for a fight at this point if, without even beginning to look for the lost object (and possibly without even looking up from her magazine), she replies either (a) 'why do you need it?' (b) 'I don't even know *what* it is, how would I know *where* it is' or, worst of all, (c) 'where did you put it?' 2. the act of having sex with a single woman; since Women's Lib, frequently referred to as Ms. lay. 3. also, the act of having sex with someone in a dark room and discovering later that you laid the wrong person – a discovery which is particularly traumatic if it turns out that your partner was somebody who (a) is related to you, (b) is of the wrong gender, (c) is of the wrong species,

	or (d) was still in the bathroom getting ready after you had already finished.
Misunderstanding	any understanding between a man and woman.
Monologue	1. a type of conversation engaged in by a man, which he later refers to as brilliant and stimulating. 2. a woman's part of the conversation when she and a man are discussing marriage, commitment and the future.
Monotone	the way a woman talks when she is angry with a man, characterized by a flat delivery devoid of effect. If she keeps this up for several days or weeks, the man with whom she is angry will finally notice that something is wrong and ask, 'Did you get your hair cut or something?'
Monotony	the part of a relationship that begins immediately after the anxiety and discomfort, which characterize the first phase, subside.
Mope	to wander about, appearing

Mope (cont'd.)	dispirited, listless and apathetic. This is an especially effective technique when used by a woman in the early part of a relationship, at which time her partner will do almost anything to raise her low spirits. Later in a relationship, this technique is seldom effective, since the man either doesn't notice or else assumes that she is thinking about what to fix for dinner.
Mother	the first woman in a man's life; he loves and hates her, complains about being babied by her and complains when he's not, and constantly rejects her love, only to then try to win it back – thus setting the stage for all of his future relationships with women. By discovering what a man's mother is like, a woman can thereby hopefully avoid the two catastrophic mistakes that nearly every woman in a relationship makes: (1) being like his mother and (2) not being like his mother.
Mr. Right	a man a woman barely knows or

	can't have. Also, a man a woman had at one time and got rid of, who now is in love with somebody else.
Music	loud noise in a singles bar, designed to make it impossible for clientele to talk with each other; the goal is to keep customers from leaving by preventing them from discovering that all the people in the bar to whom they're attracted are either married or stupid or both.
Mystery	something that attracts curiosity and speculation but defies explanation and cannot be fully understood by human reason, as in any interaction between a man and a woman.

N

Nagging	the discussion of problems in a relationship, involving the woman doing the talking. When the man does the talking, it is called problem solving or clearing the air.
Natural	a type of look that takes two hours and £20 worth of cosmetics to achieve.
Negative	possessing an attitude of doubt, cynicism, and scepticism; it is frequently attributed to women in their relationships with men, in which case the word negative is synonymous with the words realistic and experienced.
Neglect	to pay attention to one's wife or steady girlfriend in the manner to which she will become accustomed.
Neighbours	the people living near a person; in a singles complex, where a woman has

Neighbours (cont'd.) moved to meet new, eligible men, the neighbours in her building usually consist of (a) a newlywed couple next door, (b) two gay guys living together downstairs, (c) a 300-pound maniacal man upstairs who is on the make, and (d) nineteen other single women who are fighting over (c).

Nervous Breakdown an emotional disorder characterized by impaired interpersonal functioning fatigue, depression, headaches, hypersensitivity and psychosomatic disorders. It is synonymous with the less professional terms 'going bonkers', 'being off your rocker' and 'being in love'.

Neurotic a man's word for the type of woman who gets upset if a man cheats on his taxes, drives on the wrong side of the street or parks illegally. Such neurotic behaviour in women is based on the underlying neurotic belief held by most women that it is illegal to break the law.

Newspaper a paper that is printed and distributed regularly, from which a man reads aloud stock quotations, business news, and sports statistics to a bored and impatient woman, who just wants to know her horoscope and whether Selfridges is having a sale.

Nickname a cute, affectionate name that a man has for a woman and that is usually related to some flaw she has and about which she is extremely sensitive. Examples include an overweight woman being called 'Chubby' or 'Fatso', a woman with acne being called 'Zit-face', and a woman, who is not very intelligent being called 'Dumbo'.

Nightcrawler 1. a large worm used by males either as bait or as a means of getting a reaction from females, particularly those who are nervous or easily frightened. Possibly due to such usage, psychologists refer to worms and other snake-like creatures as phallic symbols. 2. a man who, following an unsuccessful night at the singles bars, calls an old girlfriend at midnight and begs her to take him back.

Nitpicker	a word used by men to describe (a) a woman who refuses to date a man simply because he is grossly overweight, boring, unemployed and already married, or (b) a man who complains because his date, who has huge boobs, is stupid, superficial and a poor conversationalist.
Nymphomaniac	a man's term for a woman who wants to have sex more often than he does.

O

Obsession	a mental state, wherein the thought of a person has more impact than the actual person. In extreme cases, one does not even recognize the loved one when encountered on the street. The prevalence of this condition is evidenced in the popular cliché, 'Absence makes the heart grow fonder'.
Open Marriage	a marriage wherein the man is free to sleep with anyone of his choosing, as long as his wife doesn't find out.
Optimist	a woman who believes that her date's failure to show up means that he's deathly ill or was in a car accident; if he never calls again, she assumes that he died without ever having regained consciousness.
Organized Religion	what a man who hates to get up early on Sunday mornings doesn't believe in.

Outdoor Barbecuing the only type of cooking that a 'real' man will do. When a man volunteers to do such cooking, the following chain of events is put in motion: (1) the woman goes to the store; (2) the woman fixes the salad, vegetables and dessert; (3) the woman prepares the meat for cooking, places it on a tray along with the necessary cooking utensils, and takes it to the man, who is lounging beside the grill, drinking a beer; (4) the man places the meat on the grill; (5) the woman goes inside to set the table and check the vegetables; (6) the woman comes out to tell the man that the meat is burning; (7) the man takes the meat off the grill and hands it to the woman; (8) the woman prepares the plates and brings them to the table: (9) after eating, the woman clears the table and does the dishes; (10) the man asks the woman how she enjoyed her 'night off' and, upon seeing her annoyed reaction, concludes that there's just no pleasing some women.

Out-of-the-Way Spot a quite, dimly-lit place where a man takes a woman so that they can be alone – and so that they won't run into friends of his wife (or steady girlfriend). A good rule of thumb is: whenever the time it takes to get to an 'out-of-the-way spot' exceeds the time spent there, it is doubtful that the main attraction is the food.

P

Panic — the state in which any available member of the opposite sex suddenly seems highly appealing, often noted in single women as their thirty-fifth birthday approaches or two weeks prior to New Year's Eve and in men at a bar shortly before closing time.

Penis Envy — a term used to describe a woman's desire to have the basic attributes of a man. Statistics indicate that penis envy is nearly as prevalent as Herpes Envy and Pimple Envy.

Penis Size — the most important statistic of all those with which a man is obsessed, far outweighing even such other crucial numerical facts as his girlfriend's chest size and the Queen's income tax liability. While methods of measurement vary, the most accepted method is for the man to

Penis Size (cont'd.)	measure the distance from his navel to the tip of his penis and then add three inches.

Personal Ads	a form of advertisement that is popular with female readers, since it gives them advance information as to how a prospective date will later perform such important dating-related male functions as lying, exaggerating and miscommunicating. The following guidelines exist in terms of translating a man's personal ad:

Describes Self As . . .	*Translation:*
1. mature	He's 89 years old.
2. tired of the bar scene.	He's already made out with all the women in all the bars.
3. educated.	He attended primary school.
4. honest.	He'll never hesitate to tell you everything

	that's wrong with you.
5. financially secure.	He currently receives unemployment benefit, in addition to alimony from his ex-wife.
Seeks Woman Who . . .	*Translation:*
1. is discreet	He's married.
2. wants 50–50 relationship	He doesn't want to pay for your dinner.
3. likes children	He has custody of his six teenage children and wants you to stay with them while he goes on holiday.
4. likes animals	He wants to videotape you having sex

Personal Ads (cont'd.)		with his German Shepherd.
	5. likes the outdoors	He wants you to do his gardening.
	6. is free on weekends for travel and recreation	He wants you to take his kids to their school matches on Saturday and Sunday.
	7. likes sports	He wants you to bring him beer and crisps while he watches football on TV.

Pessimist	a woman who has been single for a long time and dated a lot of men.
Pimples	the feature generally referred to when the writer of a personal ad describes his appearance as 'youthful'.

Playing Deaf a popular game between a man and a woman, in which the man pretends not to have heard something the woman has said. If the woman's comment involves a request or reminder, the woman's next move is to either (a) repeat her statement, in which case she is accused of nagging, or (b) say nothing, in which case she is accused of deliberately letting the man miss a hot meal, an important appointment, etc. In another variation of the game, in which the woman's initial speech involves relating an incident which she finds interesting or amusing, the man generally waits until the end of the woman's narration, pauses for a moment, and then asks her to repeat what she said. A skilled female player often simply refuses to do so, leading to the man's accusation that she is irritable, followed by termination of further play. A less experienced female player (or one who is afraid of appearing irritable) may repeat herself, in which case the man is allowed to go to Phase Two, called Playing Dumb, in which he pretends to be unable either to

Playing Deaf (cont'd)	understand the point of the story or to remember the people, places and events which are essential to appreciating it.
Poor Sport	1. a woman who becomes angry when she discovers that she was being videotaped by a hidden camera in the bathroom. 2. a man's critique of any sport that women enjoy and men don't such as shopping, sunbathing and talking on the telephone.
Potato Crisps	the hors d'oeuvres served at a dinner party given by a man.
Powder Puff Mechanics	a course taken by a woman that enables her to more adequately deal with routine and emergency car repairs. A female graduate of a powder puff mechanics course can be readily identified since she, unlike other women, is competent and in charge when confronted with such emergencies as a flat tyre; in fact, once the 'powder puff mechanic' has flagged down a man to change her tyre, she is even able to answer the inevitable, dreaded

question (always posed by male tyre-changers in an effort to humiliate female drivers): 'Do you know where the jack is?' This awareness of jack location serves three important functions for the liberated female driver: (1) it conveys to the man who is changing her tyre that she is self-sufficient and can take care of herself; (2) it allows her to more intelligently direct and criticize the work he is doing; and (3) it enables her to more completely fulfil the universal criterion which states that a woman should always be able to locate any object for which a man is looking.

P.R. the act of spending an excessive amount of time eating, drinking, and flirting – and later referring to it as work. P.R. (short for Partying Responsibility) usually constitutes 50–95 percent of a man's job.

Premarital Counselling professional guidance in handling a relationship, designed to prepare soon-to-be-married couples for divorce.

Premenstrual Syndrome

chronic irritability in a woman that usually occurs the week prior to her period, causing her to engage in such irritable behaviour as (a) frowning when a man burns a hole in her sofa, (b) not laughing when he playfully throws her to the floor and dislocates her shoulder, and (c) saying 'no' when he comes in at three a.m. with beer on his breath and lipstick on his underwear and asks her if she's in the mood for sex. While the causes of premenstrual syndrome are not well understood, it has been found to be more prevalent in women who are married to salesmen and practical jokers, and tends to disappear when women are placed in settings where there are no men.

Principles of Driving

driving standards practised by men in an effort to make driving more challenging, more competitive, and more frightening to their female passengers. The following guidelines exist:

Speed – Always drive at least 20 miles over the speed limit unless you are late for an event that is important to your female passenger, in which case you should drive very slowly, point out the scenery along the journey, and stop on the way to check your oil and put air in your tyres.

Attention – Make sure that you have enough gadgets in your car to ensure that you will seldom have time to look at the road; if you must look outside the car, concentrate on staring at women in other cars or on trying to read the bumper sticker on the car in front of you, which says something like, 'If you can read this, you're following too closely.'

Turning – Always turn right (even if your destination is to the left); this is particularly challenging (and therefore desirable) at those times when a right turn requires crossing several lanes of traffic and driving over a concrete median in the centre of the road (If your female passenger turns pale, covers her eyes and screams, you can be certain that you are practising good competitive driving).

Parking – Never park in a legitimate space unless all the handicapped and

Principles of Driving (cont'd.)	bus lane spaces are taken. *Stoplight* –Whenever you see an amber light, even if it is two miles ahead, step on the accelerator and go through the crossing without stopping. While the light may be red when you actually arrive at the intersection, what counts is that it was amber at the time that the decision not to stop was initially made. *Exit* – Never move from the far right lane of a motorway until your exit is less than five feet ahead, so that you are required to make a 90° turn across three lanes of congested traffic. A reliable clue that it is almost time to start thinking about getting over is when your female passenger says, 'You just missed our exit'.
Privileged Information	the principle that dictates certain information should not be shared with others. It is this principle that compels a man to engage in behaviours which seem simply illegal or irritating to women, who tend to lack the strong political convictions of men and, hence, to misunder-

stand when a man is behaving in a politically motivated manner. Examples of male behaviours that are based on the privileged information doctrine, and which tend to be misunderstood, include: (a) lying to the Inland Revenue, (b) failing to divulge one's true martial status to single women in bars; and (c) refusing to use a turn signal when driving, based on the male driver's contention that it's nobody else's business where he's going anyway.

Psychological Warfare the process of using psychological jargon to win an argument, thereby giving the advantage to any person who is in therapy or who has training in psychology. An example is a woman telling a man with whom she is arguing, 'Your problem is that you are a narcissistic mysogynist who overuses displacement and is fixated in the oral stage on psychosexual development.'

Q

Qualification a modification, limitation or restriction added by a man to a statement that without the modification would contain some type of commitment, promise or meaning. Examples include the following:

Statement:	*Qualification:*
1. 'I'll call you tomorrow.'	'. . . unless something comes up.'
2. 'I want you to marry me.'	'. . . but I don't deserve someone as great as you.'
3. 'I promise it won't happen again.'	'. . . if I can help it.'

Questionnaire a list of questions, often found in women's magazines, used to gain statistical information, to obtain opinions and to depress the reader

Questionnaire (cont'd.)	by subsequently releasing results that show she is above average in such categories as age and weight and below average in such categories as income, education and orgasms per week.
Quiz	1. a series of questions, usually in a women's magazine, which are answered by the reader and yield a score that generally indicates she should abandon a relationship, job or lifestyle, which she already possesses and previously thought she enjoyed, in order to pursue one that is less fun and/or less available – based on the saying 'A bird in the bush is worth two in the hand'. 2. a series of questions used by a person meeting new members of the opposite sex or one trying to get the truth about where a spouse or boyfriend was the previous night, usually yielding a pass-fail rather than a numerical score and most valid when not anticipated by the examinee, as in a Pop Quiz.

R

Radar Detector	a device that signals that a police car is in the vicinity, thereby alerting the male driver who is in a 35 mile-per-hour zone that it is time to slow down to 50 miles per hour.
Rationale	the reason behind an unreasonable order given by one person to another. Those women who, in childhood, unquestioningly accepted the usual rationale given by parents and teachers, tend to do better later in their dealings with husbands, boyfriends and male bosses, since they are less resistant to the rationale 'Because I said so'.
Reappraisal	the process of re-evaluating traits in one's partner that initially seemed positive and valuable, but which in reappraisal are exposed for the annoying habits they really are. For example:

Reappraisal (cont'd.)	Seemed to Be . . .	Is Really . . .
	observant	nosy
	bright	intellectual snob
	self-confident	conceited
	witty	ridiculous
	unique	bizarre
	reliable	boring
	affectionate	smothering
	successful	materialistic
	involved	obsessed

Rebuttal a man's response to any opinion that his date or spouse expresses.

Recliner 1. the chair in which a man sleeps in that period of time between the conclusion of dinner and the moment when his female partner wakes him to tell him that it's time for bed. 2. a man who is at home but not at the dinner table.

Reconciliation an act that gave rise to the saying, 'History repeats itself'.

Rehearsal a man's first marriage

Relationship the process of giving up those people who share your interests,

	humour and habits in order to spend more time with someone who doesn't.
Relationship Analysis	the process of two or more women spending three hours discussing and analyzing a two-minute conversation that one of them had with a man.
Remote Control	1. an energy-saving device that allows a man to (a) watch three sporting events at one time, (b) quickly change stations whenever his female companion becomes interested in a programme, and (c) transform television-watching into an event comparable to staring at a strobe light. It is considered an energy-saving device because it allows a man to completely irritate the woman in his life without even expending the energy required to get up from his chair or to open his mouth. 2. a woman's method of controlling and manipulating a man through employment of such techniques as the 'silent treatment', prolonged moping and sexual withdrawal.

Replay — the playing over of a television tape, often in slow motion, directly following the live occurrence, particularly during sporting events. The replay gives the male viewer the opportunity to frantically and urgently shout for the female non-viewer in the next room, who, in her alarm, drops what she is doing (which usually involves something breakable) and runs into the TV room to see what the emergency is; she usually arrives just in time to observe the brunt of the violence, aggressiveness and craziness (both on TV and in her mate's behaviour) which she was in the next room trying to avoid. The replay is thought by many to be responsible for instilling in the male mind the drive for repetition, thereby accounting for such behaviours as telling the same joke or story repeatedly, using the same line over and over, and attempting to reconcile with ex-wives or old girlfriends.

Repetition — an act exhibited by a man after a woman tells him that she has

	already heard the joke or story which he is about to tell her.
Rhetorical Question	a question asked merely for effect, with no answer being expected, as when a woman asks a question to a man who is watching a football game or reading a newspaper.
Ride Home	Something offered by a man to a woman, generally without mentioning the fact that the ride is to *his* home.
Rival	a woman's adversary in competing for a man. A successful rival is easy to spot, as she is (a) less interested in the man than you are during the competition and (b) totally disinterested in him following the competition.
Room-mate	a synonym for the word 'wife', generally used by a man when describing his living situation to an attractive single woman, who wants to know why they can't go to his place instead of hers.

Ruined an excellent, guilt-provoking word to use during arguments. For example, if a man drops a potato chip on the sofa, a good response is, 'You've *ruined* the sofa', or if he's ten minutes late for a sandwich dinner, an effective reprimand is 'Dinner is *ruined*!' At other times relatively minor events, which sound unimportant if spoken, can be met with the more general response, 'Now you've ruined *everything*!'

Run-on Sentence 1. a person's method of talking to an attractive member of the opposite sex, when the latter is obviously waiting for a break in the conversation, in order to make a polite exit. 2. a term used by men to describe any marriage that lasts more than a year.

S

Sadomasochist	one who enjoys both inflicting and experiencing pain; this type of person usually enjoys dating and being in love.
Secondary Gain	a phenomenon in which a person's behaviour not only results in the expected, obvious pleasure but also has a secondary reward. An example is a man experiencing the basic satisfaction of emitting a loud, lengthy belch, while simultaneously gaining the added pleasure of irritating and embarrassing his female companion.
Self-congratulatory Statement	the type of statement made by a man in response to a remarkable, difficult task performed by a woman. An example is a woman preparing a delicious seven-course meal for a man, only to have him respond to her request for feedback with a statement such as, 'You know

Self-congratulatory Statement (cont'd.)	me – I'm easy to please', or 'I'm agreeable – I like just about any thing'.
Sensitivity	a trait attributed to men who cry in front of women. Recently many highly insensitive men have developed this skill, having realized that in the era of the new woman it is more of a turn-on than crushing beer cans in their bare hands. A good rule of thumb is: never trust a man who cries on the first date.
Separation	a term meaning that a man and his wife are separated. While a woman hearing the term defines it as the period of living apart prior to divorce, the man using it often means that he is out drinking and his wife is home with the kids.
Sexy	the way a dress looks on a stranger which on a man's date or spouse would be called vulgar.
Sexual Discrimination	the situation in which an individual is unfairly denied access to certain rights, opportunities and jobs

because of his or her sex. Such discrimination affects men as well as women, as noted in the following examples of jobs that are dominated by one sex, to the unfair exclusion of the other:

Male-Dominated Jobs:
1. flying jet airplanes
2. running a major corporation
3. serving in Parliament

Female-Dominated Jobs:
1. washing dishes
2. hanging up clothes
3. cleaning toilets

Sexual Preparation those activities that a woman performs in the bathroom while her male partner is ready and waiting in the bedroom. The quantity of these activities increases proportionately not only to the compulsive nature of the woman, but also to the amount of irritation she has felt toward her male partner in the past twenty-four hours. These bathroom activities often include, but are not limited to, the following: (1) brushing teeth, (2) donning sexy nightgown, (3) putting on perfume, (4) plucking eyebrows,

Sexual Preparation (cont'd.)	(5) shaving legs, (6) polishing fingernails, (7) scrubbing bathroom floor, (8) cleaning toilet, (9) rearranging articles in medicine cabinet, and (10) putting up new wallpaper.
Sharing Household Chores	a new concept, brought about by the prevalence of working women, in which a man who lives with a woman assumes responsibility for many of the household duties. The division of chores generally falls along lines similar to the following:

Woman's Chore:	*Man's Chore:*
1. cooks food	1. eats food
2. washes clothes	2. dirties clothes
3. cleans toilet	3. uses toilet
4. washes dishes	4. eats on dishes
5. makes bed	5. sleeps in bed

Siesta	the afternoon activity of a salesman whose office is in his home.
Single	a self-descriptive term used by a man in a conversation with a single

	woman, meaning that his wife is not in the room.
Singles Bar	1. a place where single women gather to meet single, available men. 2. also, a place where married men gather for the purpose of pretending to be single and available.
Singles Complex	1. apartments that are designed for singles. Many advertise that they are for 'mature' or 'sophisticated' adults; this means that you must have enough money to pay the rent. 2. a psychological condition in which a person feels self-conscious and anxious regarding being unmarried. This condition is most prevalent in single women during parental visits or phone calls, chance meetings with recently married ex-boyfriends and twenty-year school reunions.
Singlewoman Law of Attending Parties	the only party all year to which you bring a date will also be the only party where there is abundance of attractive, eligible men.

Singlewoman Law of Attending Parties Corollary unless you really like the man you're with, in which case, for every man, there will be ten gorgeous, available women, all of whom are making a play for your date.

Sixth Sense 1. the ability of a woman to pick up on subtle cues, which a man misses, such as when she realizes (but he doesn't) that (a) his secretary who calls in sick twice a week, while coming in late and leaving early on other days, is taking advantage of him, (b) his friend who is falling over furniture, spilling drinks and slurring his words has had too much to drink, and (c) that 19-year-old woman in the seductive, low-cut dress, who gives every man at the party a long, lingering hello kiss is not an innocent girl who's just being friendly. 2. the ability of a man to sense (a) what a woman is serving for dinner, so that he can have the same thing for lunch, and (b) when a woman has just finished with a chore, so that he can offer to help.

Ski Club a club made up primarily of single people who attend the meetings in order to meet members of the opposite sex; few ski club members actually ski; though many of them wear ski clothing and a few of them have actually seen snow.

Sleazy a word used to describe an attractive woman, by a man who can't have her or a woman who is in competition with her.

'Smile' the word 95 out of 100 men say (instead of hello) when walking past a woman in a bar, regardless of whether the woman is already smiling or, conversely, has no reason to smile. This has replaced 'Don't I know you?' and 'What's your sign?' as the number one line, not only in terms of frequency but also in terms of irritating quality. Men who use the 'smile' line tend to be equally positive and compassionate in their more intimate relationships, often utilizing helpful techniques as advising a woman who is having a nervous breakdown to 'relax' or one who just attempted suicide to 'cheer up'.

Sober	a condition in which it is almost impossible to fall in love.
Space	a term meaning less crowded, implying more room for oneself; when a man in a relationship asks for more space, it is generally not to be alone or less crowded, but rather to have the opportunity to share his space with somebody new.
Spectator	a man who is helping a woman clean house, do dishes or prepare a meal.
Speed Limit	a law regarding how fast motorists are allowed to drive. This law does not apply to people on important official business who have had practice driving recklessly at high speeds, including policemen, firemen and men in general.
Spot Reducing	the phenomenon of losing weight in only certain specific parts of the body, most likely to affect woman's breasts, hair and fingernails, and least likely to affect her hips thighs, and stomach.

Storage — the process of storing material for later use, as when a woman stores up every mistake and indiscretion made by a man, for use when arguing with him hours, days or even years later.

Starting a Fight — a skill that is honed to perfection as a relationship progresses. With practice, one can learn to turn nearly any event or comment into a source of conflict, as in the following examples:

Man's Comment:	*Woman's Response:*
1. 'I like your hair like that.'	'You don't like it the way I usually wear it?'
2. 'This steak is great!'	'What's wrong with the potato?'
3. 'Your sister seems nice.'	'Oh yeah – take *her* side!'
4. Where would you like to go?'	'How come I always have to

Starting a Fight (cont'd.)		make all the decisions?!'
	5. 'Let's go to the cinema.'	'How come I never get to make any of the decisions?!'
	6. 'I love you.'	'What's that supposed to mean?!'
	7. ' . . . '	'How come you never talk to me any more?'

Studfinder 1. a mechanical device for locating studs in a wall, generally used only by unskilled men who don't possess the knack for using the more popular, masculine technique involving (a) tapping various places on the wall, (b) confidently making a large hole by hammering a huge bolt or nail into the wall, (c) hanging a heavy picture on the nail, (d) waiting for the picture, nail, and a large portion of the wall to fall off, and (e) repeating

	(a) through (d). 2. a woman who is successful at locating the interesting men in a singles bar.
Stylish	a word used to describe the type of female clothing that men hate.
Supermarket	a popular meeting place for singles, many of whom push empty trolleys around the place and ask attractive members of the opposite sex where certain items are shelved or how to prepare a particular food. This is very irritating to the few people in the store who are really shopping and to the check-out staff and shelf-stackers who are not yet comfortable with the task of approaching female customers and saying, 'The gentleman over there would like to buy you a jar of Hellman's Mayonnaise.'
Swimming Pool	a body of water at a singles complex, designed for the purpose of placing lounge chairs around it. Nobody actually uses the water for swimming, as the men want to avoid getting their hair wet and the women are generally wearing

Swimming Pool (cont'd.)	swimsuits that will shrink, fade or fall apart if immersed in water.
Sympathetic Response	1. those physiological reactions associated with falling in love, which are so exhilarating and so enjoyable that, by comparison, any flaw in the loved one seems inconsequential and unimportant. Such pleasurable sensations include sweaty palms, pounding heart, upset stomach, muscular tension, elevated blood pressure, irritability, inability to concentrate, and general feelings of dizziness and nausea. 2. a compassionate response that in the early part of a dating relationship tends to be superficial and patronizing, but which, with time, becomes more honest, natural, and spontaneous, as in the following examples:

Statement:	*Response (on fifth date):*	*Response (on fiftieth date):*
1. 'I'm so tired. Do you mind eating in?'	'Of course not. I love cooking for you.'	'What do you think this is – a restaurant?'
2. 'I've had a terrible day!'	'Let me get you a drink	'You had a terrible day! Let me tell

	and then you can tell me all about it.'	you about *mine!*'
3. 'I'm sorry to ramble on like this. You must be tired of listening to all my problems.'	'Not at all. It makes me feel closer to you.'	'. . . Do you mind if I turn up the TV volume?'
4. 'I'm afraid that it wasn't very good for you.'	'It was wonderful.'	'You mean you're *done*? I didn't know we'd even started!'

T

Table Manners	those rules of etiquette that govern a woman's dining behaviour, and which, in modified form, are also practised by male diners. The following rules and male amendments to the rules apply:
Rule:	*Male Amendment:*
1. Do not take the last remaining piece of meat	. . . if it is currently being eaten by anyone other than your date.
2. Do not talk with your mouth full	. . . unless your mouth happens to be full when you suddenly recall a very gross, dirty joke that you need to tell immediately.
3. Do not comment on the origin of the meat that is being served	. . . unless you have some interesting, first-hand information, such as gory stories about the time you visited a slaughterhouse.
4. Do not ask what a dish is,	. . . except to make sure that the little black things are not bugs, the

Table Manners (cont'd.) if you don't recognize it	long, stringy stuff is not hair, and the indistinguishable meat is not animal brains or intestines.
5. Do not spit out a tough piece of meat.	. . . unless you can subsequently justify your behaviour by locating the offending gristle, bone or fat and showing the proof to your fellow diners.
6. Do not start eating until the hostess begins	. . . unless you are obviously much hungrier than she is.
7. Do not comment on how many calories are in the food	. . . unless there are some overweight people at the table, to whom you can then turn and say, 'But I guess you never worry about that, do you?'
8. Do not ask if there is more in the kitchen	. . . until after you have finished all the food on your plate, your date's plate, and the plate of anyone else whom you know on a first-name basis.

Telephone	an apparatus used by a man for waking a woman up or getting her out of the bathtub, in order to confirm a time at which he later

won't show up for a date.

Telephone Answering Machine 1. an apparatus attached to a phone, giving callers one is hoping to hear from the opportunity to snicker at how the person being called sounds on tape, prior to hanging up without leaving a message. 2. an instrument of torture owned by a single woman, allowing her to experience a brief period of excitement upon discovering that she had twelve phone calls while she was gone; this quickly gives way to her extreme depression when she plays back the messages and discovers that (a) six are from an obnoxious man whom she thought she was finally rid of, (b) one is from the dentist telling her that, upon re-examining her X-rays, he has discovered that she needs root canal treatment of £300, (c) one is from the mechanic who has been working on her car, telling her that he had to replace a valve in her vehicle, the cost of which is more than the value of the car, and (d) four are from her mother asking why she never came home all night.

Ten a numerical rating implying perfection, assigned by men judging women; a ten is what every man, regardless of his own level of imperfection, feels that he deserves. A woman's rating is immediately reduced by four points if the male judge discovers that she is either intelligent or available.

Therapist a professional who, for money, will listen sympathetically and supportively for hours to stories about a person's unhappy love life; his services are especially essential as people grow older and their friends begin to think that they've heard all this before.

Three-Piece Suit the clothing that a man runs home to change into, prior to stopping by the local singles bar on his way home from work.

Timing 1. an important variable that draws two people together, meaning that they are both available and ready at the same time, as when a woman who has just broken up with her boyfriend meets a man whose wife is out of town. 2. the tendency of a man who has already finished, to keep track of how long he must wait for his partner to finish, when performing such behaviours as shopping, getting dressed and having sex.

Tomorrow a time concept upon which men and women often disagree. To most men, tomorrow means some time in the future; this leads to frequent difficulties with less flexible linguists (i.e., women), who develop unrealistic expectations when hearing such sentences as 'I'll call you tomorrow' or 'I'll pay you back tomorrow'.

Too Young 1. a man who is more than five years younger than his female date. 2. a woman who is more than five years younger than her male date's granddaughter.

Trust a concept implying faith and confidence; its presence in a relationship seems to be especially important to those men who are the most difficult to trust. Hence, when a man comes home at three a.m., having mis-

Trust (cont'd.)	placed his tie, watch and underwear, and finds his mate waiting up, it is typical for him to angrily make the accusation, 'You don't trust me!' Likewise, when caught in bed with another woman, it is not unusual for the man to self-righteously inform the betrayed woman that now he has proof and knows for sure that she is checking up on him and doesn't trust him.
Tummy Tuck	1. the operation referred to but not directly mentioned when a flat-tummied spokesperson, who is promoting an exercise programme, exercise tape or exercise book claims, 'You can look like me in a just a few short weeks.' 2. the reflex action exhibited by a person in a swimsuit when walking past one or more members of the opposite sex.

U

Ultimatum	a popular strategy for eliminating unwanted behaviours, used by parents, bosses, and men and women in relationships; it involves making a demand and stating a dire consequence that will occur if that demand is not met. In terms of preventing an unwanted behaviour from being exhibited, this tactic is nearly as effective as the phrase, 'I dare you'.
Unclear	a type of language used by lawyers, car mechanics, and men talking to women, in an attempt to get the listener to agree to something that is in the best interests of the speaker.
Understanding	a word men use to describe the perfect woman, meaning that she does not get upset when he is two hours late for a date, forgets her birthday or flirts outrageously with other women. In reality, if a man is

Understanding (cont'd.)	involved with a woman who is this calm and understanding, she is also either on drugs, extremely desperate or in love with somebody else.
Unexpressed Feelings	1. in a man, all feelings except anger. 2. in a woman, those feelings that she has when alone in a house where the phone is out of order.
Upper Hand	the person in a relationship who doesn't have to turn out the lights at bedtime, listen when the other person talks, or relinquish the position with the better view in a restaurant, at a football match or during sex.

V

VCR	an electronic device that allows a man to tape a sporting event, so that he can watch the same play over and over, rather than being limited to seeing it only during live coverage, instant replays, the sports round-up, satellite broadcast, *Sportsnight*, and the pre-game rundown of the following week's game.
Velocity	the measurement of speed, considered by most men to be the primary measure of how well they are doing on such tasks as driving, drinking, eating and sexual performance.
Victim	a woman who works for, is romantically involved with, or uses the professional services of a man.
Virgin	the type of woman a man would never date but expects to marry.

Visitation an event that occurs on a regular basis, usually every other weekend, in which a woman's divorced boyfriend's two children move in with him for the weekend and she comes to babysit for the three of them.

W

Waffle	one of the many treats a 95-pound single woman passes up, so that her 275-pound boyfriend won't think she's getting fat.
Waiter	a man a single woman meets in a bar who tells her he is in the restaurant business.
Washing Machine	what a woman turns into when she moves in with a man.
Waterbed	a bed in a bachelor's apartment, which is popular with men because it (a) makes it difficult for a woman to get out of bed once she is in it, (b) generates maximum motion with minimum effort, and (c) creates a feeling of seasickness and nausea, which they hope their female bed-partners will confuse with love, since the two feel much the same.

Watermelon	a man's opinion of the ideal female breast size.
WATS Line	1. a US telephone line allowing a business that makes lots of long-distance phone calls to save money on those calls, especially practical in companies where the executives have an abundance or out-of-town girlfriends; this is a service much envied by many men in the UK. 2. one of a number of popular lines used in a singles bar, including, 'What's your name?', 'What's your sign?', 'What's your income?', and 'What's your bra size?' 3. also, those lines are used later in a relationship, the most popular of which are, 'What's for dinner?', 'What's your problem?', and 'What's happened to your hair?'
Whiplash	a condition suffered by men sitting at a bar with their backs to a roomful of women.
'Why?'	a popular stalling technique utilized by the guilty party in an argument between a man and a woman. Polls indicate that 'why?' is the favoured

response of 70% of the population in response to such questions as, 'What time did you get in?', 'Where have you been?' and 'Who was that on the phone?' Other popular responses to such questions include (a) 'I resent your implication'; (b) 'If you don't trust me, we better just call this whole thing off right now'; (c) 'Never mind *me*! What about *you*?!' and (d) 'I refuse to answer without benefit of legal counsel'.

Will Rogers a man who once said, 'I never met a man I didn't like'; based on his statement, historians have been able to state, with confidence, that Will never went to a singles' bar.

Wimp a term used by a woman to describe a former boyfriend who, prior to the break-up, was referred to as sensitive.

Women Drivers! the exasperated comment made by a male driver when a female driver squeals her brakes and veers off the road in order to avoid hitting him after he has, without warning, pulled out in front of her.

Women's Liberation the movement which guaranteed women a number of rights which had previously been denied them, including the right to pay their own way, to open their own doors, to fight and die in wars, to pay alimony and to get up at 6.00 every morning to go to work. To a large extent, these rights had previously been reserved for men. Women, meanwhile, retained sole possession of those rights which had always belonged exclusively to women, including the right to cook meals, to do the dishes, to wash the clothes, to clean the toilets, and to raise the children. The essence of this movement was captured in the words of the song from a popular US TV ad glorifying women's new role: 'I can bring home the bacon . . . fry it up in a pan . . . and never, never let him forget he's a man.'

X

X Chromosome	the chromosome that is called the female sex chromosome, as it has been scientifically linked to the development of female sex organs, large breasts and a high voice suitable for whining. When studied under powerful microscopes, these tiny chromosomes have been observed to spend excessive amounts of time engaged in such activities as shopping, talking and hair-washing; however, scientists report unexplainable alterations in the functioning of the X chromosome whenever a Y chromosome is introduced, as X then abandons the other Xs, to follow after Y and clean up Y's messes.
Xerox Machine	the machine that a female 'administrative assistant' runs during that part of the day when she is not typing or answering the phone, thus fulfilling her employer's guarantee

Xerox Machine (cont'd.)	during the job interview that her job would involve more than simply typing and answering the phone.
X-Rated Film	a film in which dozens of big-breasted, long-tongued women compete for the right to service and entertain one man, who is seldom shown doing anything but simply lying back and moaning. By watching such films the male viewer is able to objectively determine how both he and his female partner measure up sexually; this type of comparative viewing inevitably leads him to two important conclusions: (1) by comparing his female partner to the women on the screen, he determines that she is, without a doubt, frigid, inhibited and underdeveloped; and (2) by comparing himself to the men on the screen, he determines that they are, without a doubt, utilizing trick photography and/or wearing fake body parts.

Y

Yawn	a man's way of laughing at a joke told by a woman.
Y Chromosome	the male sex chromosome, so named because it carries the genetic predisposition for reckless driving, excessive beer consumption, persistent lying and frequent repetition of dirty jokes. Through studying the Y chromosome under powerful microscopes, scientists have discovered two types of structural abnormalities that may effect this chromosome, with each type displaying its own unique, abnormal pattern of activity within the cell:

Type of Abnormality:	*Chromosomal Activity (Observed via Microscope):*
1. The long-tailed Y pattern (y)	swaggers during movement; genes tend to be tight-fitting; attempts to reveal long appendage to all X chromosomes.

Y Chromosome (cont'd)

2. The short-tailed Y pattern (Y)	is less prone than the long-tailed Y to flaunt mutated appendage in front of unfamiliar X chromosome; gravitates toward those X chromosomes that display clumsy locomotion suggestive of visual perceptual difficulties; is most prevalent in genetic make-up of those males who over-use such phrases as 'Bigger isn't necessarily better', and 'It's not the size of the wand – it's the expertise of the magician'.
Yoko Ono	a woman who inspired unattractive, untalented women everywhere, by landing a rich, successful, famous husband, thereby proving that love is not only blind, it is also deaf.
You	the only correct answer to a variety of questions posed by men, including (a) Who's the best lover you ever had? (b) Who do you think is the best looking man at this party? and (c) Who's that sandwich for?

Young	an adjective used by men to describe a woman who is under 18 or a man who is under 80.
Youthful	a type of appearance that only people who are not young try to achieve. While women attempt to stay youthful-looking by exercising, keeping up with styles, staying in shape and undergoing cosmetic surgery, men use the less strenuous approach of acting immature, buying expensive toys and running around with younger women.

Z

Zero Visibility	the inability to see where one is going and, more specifically, to perceive dangers, hazards and disasters that lie just ahead. This condition commonly affects pilots in fog, drivers in smog and women in love.
Zoo	a word frequently used by single people at social gatherings, particularly those who wear massive gold chains and silk shirts unbuttoned to their navels. In a crowded bar, at least one such person per hour is guaranteed to say, 'This place is a zoo.' Currently the Zoological Society is working to ban the use of this line as animals in the zoo take great offence at being compared to people in bars. If this ban is enforced, witty bar-goers will be limited in their clever repertoire to the phrases, 'This place is a circus' and 'What a meat market'.

Z-z-z-z the male part of the conversation between a man and a woman, following sex.

Nancy Linn-Desmond lives in Atlanta, Georgia, where she works as a psychologist and freelance writer. Prior to her recent marriage, she had dated for nearly twenty years, had been to forty-three singles bars, had lived at nine different adult-only complexes and had known all the words of the song 'I Will Survive'. This is her first book.